The Wishing Star

Gumipod   Keeko   Zarabel   Rardo   Kidna   Billa   Tangeline   Tibbo

Fiona Olsson and Garry Fleming

The Five Mile Press

Rardo is a clever numbat who likes to invent things.

When Rardo thinks of a new idea, his ears stand up and twitch. They twitch slowly at first, then faster and faster until he scribbles the whole idea onto his notepad.

Some of his inventions work and others don't. But no matter what, Rardo never gives up!

It was the night before Kidna's birthday and the sky was full of stars. Rardo wanted to impress Kidna by giving him the grandest gift ever! But he just couldn't work out what it should be.

"By Gooligum! That's it!" gasped Rardo suddenly.

Pointing towards the Southern Cross in the sky he exclaimed, "I'll invent a Star Catcher and catch Kidna his very own star to wish upon!"

Rardo scampered off to collect bits and pieces from the forest floor for his invention. He tinkered through the night.

In the early hours of the morning Tibbo awoke to a very loud BANG!

Making his way over to Rardo's workshop, Tibbo asked in a sleepy voice, "Is everything alright?"

"Almost there," muttered Rardo. "I'm inventing a Star Catcher to give Kidna his very own star!"

"But how will you ever catch a star from so far away?" asked Tibbo.

"Just wait and see!" said Rardo with a wink.

At sunrise, everyone gathered at the billabong to wish Kidna a happy birthday. Billa, Tibbo, Keeko and Zarabel had made termite pies, and Tangeline had baked a wild berry cake.

"Awesome!" grinned Kidna. "But where's Rardo?"

"Oh he's busy inventing something for you," mumbled Tibbo.

"I wonder what it could be?" thought Kidna.

But with a full belly, Kidna soon fell asleep under the shade of a nearby tree.

While Kidna snoozed, Billa went to see what Rardo was doing.

"Hey Rardo! What are you up to?" he asked curiously.

Without looking up, Rardo replied, "I'm making a Star Catcher!"

Billa scratched his head and said, "But Rardo, if you catch a star the night sky won't be as bright as it's meant to be."

Rardo's ears twitched, "Billa, there are MILLIONS of stars! No-one will ever notice if just one's missing."

Practising her aerial somersaults, Zarabel swooped down to take a closer look at Rardo's invention.

"What is it, Rardo?" she chirped.

"It's going to be a Star Catcher!" announced Rardo proudly.

"But Rardo, the sun is the closest star to catch, and we need the sun!" screeched Zarabel.

"I don't want to catch the sun, Zarabel," exclaimed Rardo. "I want to give Kidna a star from the Southern Cross!"

A few moments later Keeko leapt on by.

"Before you ask," sighed Rardo, "I'm building a Star Catcher to catch a star from the Southern Cross."

"But Rardo, every night I look up at the Southern Cross," squeaked Keeko. "If you take one of its stars it won't look like a cross anymore!"

"Keeko, it's only the tiny star," groaned Rardo. "Don't worry!"

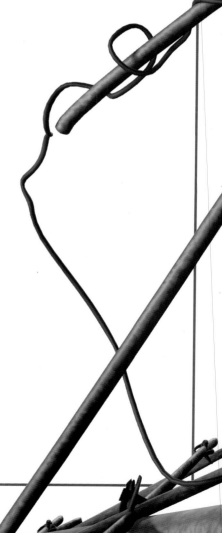

Tangeline decided it was her turn to visit Rardo.

"Do you need any help Rardo?" she asked politely.

"No, I'm fine, thank you," replied Rardo. "The Star Catcher is almost ready!"

Tangeline looked worried. "But Rardo, on our night adventures we navigate using the stars. If you take one … we'll get totally lost!"

Rardo's ears twitched. "Tangeline, I can show you plenty of other stars that we can use to find our way."

Finally at sunset Rardo was finished. He wasted no time tying the Star Catcher to the Gumipod.

It was made from hundreds of long sticks held together using gumnuts, vines and blueberry syrup. There was a rake made from twigs, a net woven from leaves and a special capturing box made out of paperbark.

"MAGNIFICENT!" beamed Rardo.

"Wake up Kidna!" shouted Rardo gleefully. "It's time to get your present!"

There was a buzz of excitement as everyone scrambled on board the Gumipod. With a ZIP and a ZOOM they were in the air.

They flew up towards the Saucepan, and then along the Milky Way to the Southern Cross.

"Oh Gooligum," gulped Rardo. "These stars still look a very long way off!"

But even so, Rardo quickly pulled the lever …

With a shudder and a loud whistle, the Star Catcher clawed its way towards the Southern Cross.

When Kidna realised what Rardo was doing he yelled, "STOP! You can't capture a star!"

Just then the Star Catcher began to shake. KABOOM!

Rardo's prized invention broke into pieces. His ears and tail drooped.

Turning to Kidna he said, "I just wanted to give you the grandest birthday gift ever!"

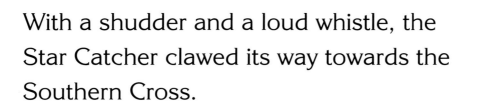

"That's a very kind thought Rardo," said Kidna, "but stars belong in the sky."

"I suppose you're right," whispered Rardo. Just then his ears started to twitch. "I know," he piped. "Let's make the Southern Cross our friendship sign!"

"Awesome!" grinned Kidna. "That way whenever we feel alone or afraid at night, we can look up and know that we have a friend."

"Now, let's go back to the tree-house and finish those termite pies!" giggled Rardo.

"Let's!" chuckled Kidna.